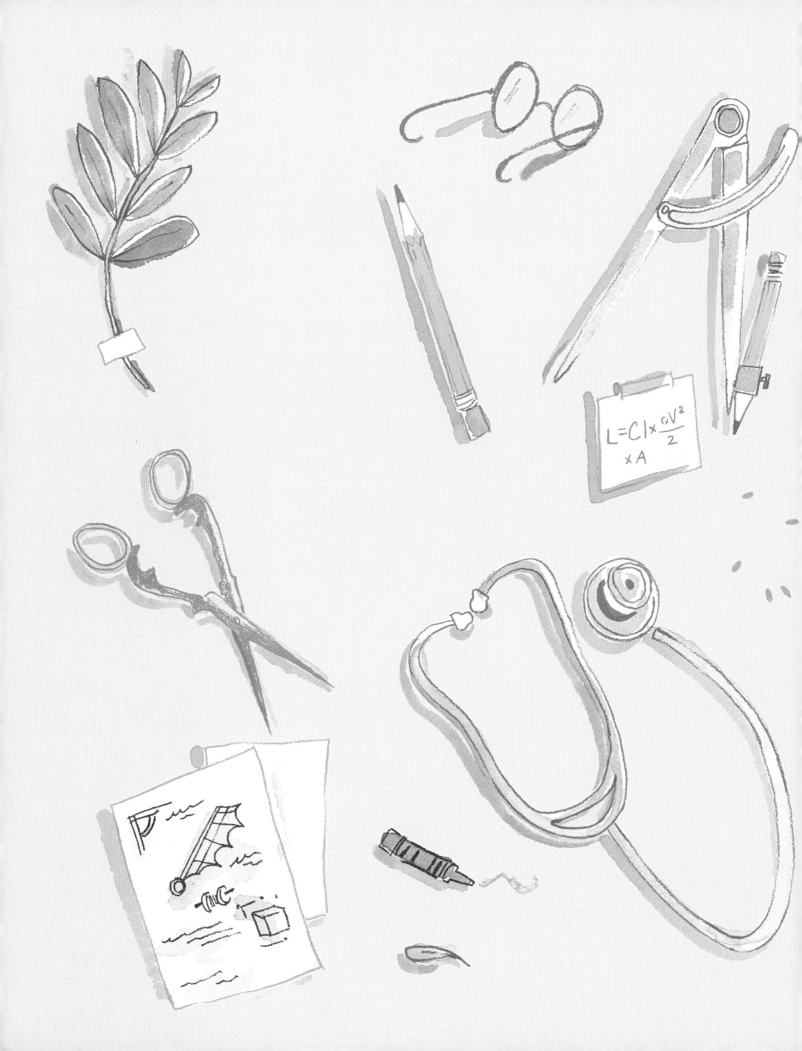

Lola Dutch
When I Grow Up

Kenneth &
Sarah Jane
Wright

BLOOMSBURY
CHILDREN'S BOOKS

LONDON OXFORD NEW YORK NEW DELHI SYDNEY

This is Lola. Lola Dutch.

Lola Dutch wants to be too much.

"Bear! We have an emergency!" said Lola. "I don't know what I want to be when I grow up!"

"That is a big decision. Should we discuss it over tea?" asked Bear.

"Oh, there's no time for that," said Lola.
"Quick, to the den!"

Bear's den was the perfect place to find inspiration. There were fascinating books on biology, astronomy and history, but today one particular book caught Lola's eye.

"That's it! I'm destined for the stage," said Lola.
"Forward, friends! We must rehearse!"

Croc built the set.

Pig composed the orchestrations.

Crane designed the costumes.

"Lola Dutch, I loved it so much!" said Bear.

"Thank you, Bear. But actually . . ."

"... I might want to be an inventor
when I grow up," said Lola.

Lola knew that to be an inventor she must . . .

research,

experiment,

improvise . . .

hypothesise,

OOPS!

and discover!
Lola's imagination . . .

... soared!

"Lola Dutch, you have learned so much," said Bear.

"But what if I'm supposed to be something else when I grow up?" Lola wondered. She took a deep breath and looked around.

Lola noticed the hum of the bees
and the fragrance of the flowers.

"Maybe I could be a botanist!" she said.

In the greenhouse . . .

Croc gathered the soil.

Pig planted the seeds.

Crane watered the seedlings.

"Bear, that's it! I will make
the earth laugh with flowers!"
Lola's ideas . . .

...blossomed.

"Lola Dutch, you've grown so much," said Bear.

"But Bear, I still can't decide what I want to be!
Maybe what I REALLY want to be is . . ."

"... a judge in the highest court."

"Or maybe an Egyptologist."

"Or an astronaut,

a pastry chef,

a veterinarian,

a safari ranger,

a yoga instructor

or a chemist?"

"But I can't decide.
It's ALL TOO MUCH!"
said Lola Dutch.

"Lola, what do you want to be right now?" asked Bear.

"I just want to be a child and learn about everything!" said Lola.

"Well then," said Bear, "I think you *should* be a child and learn about everything."

"Oh, Bear, you always know just what to say."

"I still have a little time before
I grow up, right?" asked Lola.
"Absolutely," said Bear.

"Good," said Lola, "because I have a
few more things I'd like to be tomorrow."

To our parents, who let us be kids and learn about everything

BLOOMSBURY CHILDREN'S BOOKS
Bloomsbury Publishing Plc
50 Bedford Square, London WC1B 3DP, UK

BLOOMSBURY, BLOOMSBURY CHILDREN'S BOOKS and the Diana logo
are trademarks of Bloomsbury Publishing Plc

First published in Great Britain in March 2019 by Bloomsbury Publishing Plc

First published in the USA in January 2019 by Bloomsbury Children's Books
1385 Broadway, New York, New York 10018

A catalogue record for this book is available from the British Library

ISBN 978 1 5266 0608 2

2 4 6 8 10 9 7 5 3 1

Printed in China by Leo Paper Products, Heshan, Guangdong

All papers used by Bloomsbury Publishing Plc are natural, recyclable products
from wood grown in well-managed forests. The manufacturing processes conform
to the environmental regulations of the country of origin

To find out more about our authors and books visit www.bloomsbury.com
and sign up for our newsletters

Research some of the places, characters and creators who inspired Lola Dutch: The Paris Opera House, completed 1875, designed by Charles Garnier (1825–1898) • Brünnhilde, the Valkyrie from Richard Wagner's (1813–1883) *The Ring of the Nibelung* (1876) • Leonardo da Vinci (1452–1519), artist, inventor and mathematician • Orville Wright (1871–1948) and Wilbur Wright (1867–1912) used the lift equation (wright.nasa.gov) when they invented and built the world's first successful airplane • The reference to "Earth laughs in flowers" is from the poem "Hamatreya" (1846) by Ralph Waldo Emerson (1803–1882), essayist and poet • Carrousel La Belle Époque, Place de l'Hôtel de Ville, Paris, France • Sandra Day O'Connor (b. 1930), the first woman to serve on the Supreme Court of the United States • The Great Sphinx and Pyramids (c. 2575–c. 2465 BCE), Giza, Egypt.